The Unexpected Friend

A Rohingya Children's Story

Thank you to the Rohingya children living in refugee camps in Cox's Bazar, Bangladesh. This story is inspired by you, is about you, and is for you. We are also grateful to all those who supported the development of this book with their valuable time and thoughts.

- Linda Steinbock and Eline Severijnen, Save the Children

Dedicated to children who have never seen themselves, or their stories, on the pages of a picture book.

- Raya Rahman and Inshra S Russell, Guba Publishing

Save the Children

GUBA PUBLISHING

It was the end of afternoon prayers. Faisal had just left the mosque and was waiting for his friend Rahim. Suddenly, he heard a faint chirping noise in the bushes.

He bent down and moved the leaves aside.

A small bird lay on the ground. Its wing looked broken.
Gently, Faisal picked it up.

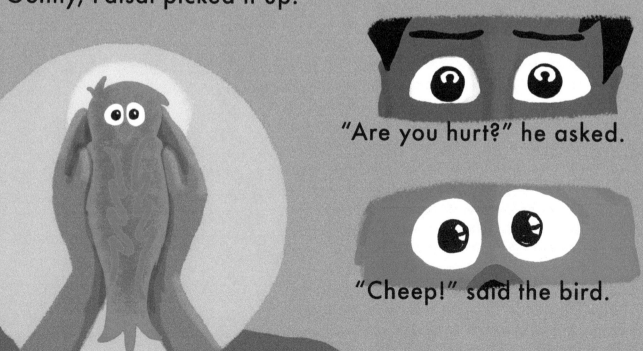

"Are you hurt?" he asked.

"Cheep!" said the bird.

"It needs help," he told Rahim. They had planned to go to the forest to get firewood after prayers. But Faisal didn't want to leave the injured bird behind.

He asked Rahim to wait for him. "I'll take it to my sisters," he explained. "They will keep it safe."

Faisal and Rahim lived in a refugee camp in Bangladesh along with many other Rohingya people. They were forced to leave their homes in Myanmar as it was no longer safe there. Faisal had walked for miles with his mother and his sisters, Rehana and Aziza, to find shelter. They arrived in this camp a while ago and stayed ever since.

Holding the bird in his cupped hands,
Faisal made his way through the camp.

He passed food lines where people waited
to receive bags of rice and cooking oil.

And he passed the busy medical clinic where many others lined up for treatment.

No doctor would have time to fix a bird there!

He reached the learning centre where his sisters and other children were drawing pictures and playing board games. "Aziza! Rehana!" he called them. "I need your help!"

The girls gasped when they looked inside the box.

"I heard it chirping by the mosque," said Faisal. "The poor thing is hurt and can't fly."

His sisters promised to take care of it. "I'll be back soon with firewood!" Faisal told them.

The forest could be scary as it was home to many wild animals. But people from the camp needed to go there to gather wood for cooking.

The boys searched for fallen twigs and branches until their arms were full. Faisal thought about the bird. Would it ever fly again?

They were about to head back when all of a sudden...

...there was a rustling noise.

It was so big! They didn't dare go any closer.
Crossing paths with an elephant could be dangerous.
Not too long ago, one had wandered into the
crowded camp and frightened everybody.

But Faisal knew that it was not the elephant's fault. After all, the forest was getting smaller as more and more trees were cut to make space for the refugee camp. He was sad that the elephant was losing its home. "Shh," whispered Rahim. "Let's leave quietly."

Lost in thought on the way back,
Faisal tripped over a big rock and fell.

"Aah, my arm!" he cried. He tried to pick up the
scattered branches but couldn't. It hurt too much.
"How will Ma cook without any firewood?"

Rahim put a hand on his shoulder.
"You can share with me," he said.

Back in the camp, Faisal was glad to see that his mother and sisters had bandaged the bird's wing. "What happened?" his mother asked him. "I fell, Ma," he said. "My arm really hurts!"

She took him inside the tent and wrapped his arm in a cotton sling. "Let's go to the clinic to make sure nothing is broken," she said softly.

Over the next few weeks, Faisal started to feel better.
The bird's wing was also healing.

They spent every minute together.

One day, the bird spread
its wings to show that it
was ready to fly.

But Faisal didn't want to let it go.

He couldn't sleep that night.
He wished they didn't have
to say goodbye.

Then he remembered his sisters' giggles,
Rahim's friendly hand on his shoulder,
and his mother's soft voice.

He had them to hold on to.

"It's time," he told his sisters the next morning.

Aziza cried the hardest. Rehana held her close. "The bird needs its family too." Faisal comforted them. "Like us," he said.

They walked to the place near the mosque where Faisal had first found the bird.

Together, they let it go. As it flew away,
they heard the call to prayer.

"Go in peace, little friend," whispered Faisal.
"I will never forget you."

Afterword

Over one million Rohingya people have fled the violence in Myanmar's Rakhine State, seeking refuge in the Cox's Bazar district of Bangladesh since early 1990. The largest exodus began on 25 August 2017, making this one of the largest humanitarian refugee crises in the world. Most refugees in Cox's Bazar are women and children, living in uncertain and difficult conditions.

Linda Steinbock and Eline Severijnen authored the report 'Childhood Interrupted: Children's Voices from the Rohingya Refugee Crisis', which inspired the creation of this book. As a child focused organisation, Save the Children believes in listening to children's experiences, needs, and hopes. The report authors were moved by the resilience in the children's stories and wanted to excite the children in the camps with a personal story about them.

Children have powerful voices. Together with you, we want to hear their message, share their stories, and raise awareness of the hopes of Rohingya children.

If you would like more information, or would like to make a contribution, please visit: https://www.savethechildren.org.uk/where-we-work/asia/rohingya-crisis

Photo credit: Leela Shafiq

Author: Raya Rahman

Raya Rahman is the cofounder and editor of a bilingual picture book company called Guba Publishing. She works in partnership with other authors, illustrators and non-profit organizations to publish diverse and multicultural children's stories and learning resources. Raya lives in Oakland, California with her husband and their two daughters.

Find her on www.instagram.com/gubapublishing

Photo credit: Gavin Fernandes

Illustrator: Inshra Sakhawat Russell

Inshra is a filmmaker, photographer and designer who loves listening to podcasts and making soup. She is the author and illustrator of "Tiny Jumps In", a picturebook about a girl who is curious about the lake she lives next to. Inshra lives in London, U.K. with her husband and their son, Ruben.

Find her swimming around in a lake of curiosity on www.instagram.com/studioinku

Photo credit: Wasfia Nazreen

Guba Publishing

Raya and Inshra have been friends since they were 8 years old. Together they established a children's publishing house called Guba Publishing to share valuable stories inspired by their Bengali roots.

If you like this book, visit our website for more diverse picture books and learning resources at www.gubapublishing.com.

Don't miss our other titles!

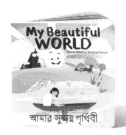

Simply visit
www.gubapublishing.com

This book was typeset in Futura Round
Medium Typeface and Mali Medium Typeface.
The illustrations were made with a drawing pencil, a scanner,
a drawing tablet, Adobe Photoshop and Adobe Illustrator.

First Edition

Library of Congress Control Number:20199
ISBN 978-1-946747-10-5 English hardcover
ISBN 978-1-946747-09-9 English paperback
ISBN 978-1-946747-11-2 Bengali paperback
ISBN 978-1-946747-12-9 Burmese paperbac

The Unexpected Friend - A Rohingya Children's Story

This illustrated story is based on a report by Linda Steinbock and Eline Severijnen titled 'Childhood Interrupted: Children's Voices from the Rohingya Refugee Crisis'.

Written by Raya Rashna Rahman | Illustrated by Inshra Sakhawat Russell

Storytelling contributions by Mitali Perkins and Inara Shafiq

Cover design and book layout by Inshra Sakhawat Russell

Bengali translation by Atiq Anan

Burmese translation by Translators without Borders

Text copyright © 2019 by Raya Rahman

Illustrations copyright © 2019 by Inshra Sakhawat Russell

CPSIA information can be obtained
at www.ICGtesting.com
Printed in the USA
LVHW072344291220
675094LV00016BA/398